UNFORTUNATE DECREES AND ICED COFFEES

A CAULDRON COFFEE SHOP STORY

LAURA GREENWOOD

Visit Laura Greenwood's website at:

www.authorlauragreenwood.co.uk

Cover by LSK Designs

Unfortunate Decrees and Iced Coffees is a work of fiction. Names, characters, places, and incidents are the products of the author's imagination or are used fictitiously. Any resemblance to actual persons, living or dead, businesses, companies, events, or locales is entirely coincidental.

If you find an error, you can report it via my website. Please note that my books are written in British English: https://www.authorlauragreenwood.co.uk/p/report-error.html

To keep up to date with new releases, sales, and other updates, you can join my mailing list via my website or The Paranormal Council Reader Group on Facebook.

BLURB

When necromancer archaeologist, Sabine, is asked to supervise an excavation of the mysterious Humber Stone, she can't resist the challenge.

But when she arrives and discovers her warlock ex is intent on stopping the dig, she realises it may be a harder task than she first thought.

The excavation may be plagued by the bad luck brought about by the stone, but at least things aren't quite so bad for Sabine's love life...

-

Unfortunate Decrees and Iced Coffees is a companion story to the *Cauldron Coffee Shop* modern fantasy series, and features an m/f romance.

1

THE EXCITEMENT of a new dig is almost too much for me to deal with. It always is. There's something about the feel of unstruck ground beneath my boots and the possibility of what's to come. It's one of the reasons I went into this line of work. The rest of it was for the adventure. There aren't many films about accountants, but there are about archaeologists.

I park my car in the designated spot and pull the door open to hop out. The team has already set up several tents, which is going to be more necessary here than in a lot of my other digs. I have the great British weather to thank for that. Even this early in the day, the wind rattles the canvas, giving the whole place a storm-tossed feel. It's oddly beautiful.

But the weather isn't why I'm here.

The Humber Stone and its mysteries beckon me, even from this distance. It might not be as visually impressive as some of the other digs I've run, but it's almost more of an enigma. No one knows what it is, or what secrets it's keeping. That's why they've called me in. They want to know, and I'm good at this kind of thing.

If I'm honest about it, there's a good chance I'm not going to be able to get to the bottom of it either. If people haven't managed for centuries, then how am I going to manage in a few weeks of digging?

I push the thought to the side. It doesn't matter if I can do it. The challenge is the same.

"Hi Sabine," Angelica says, greeting me with her trademark clipboard and a wide smile on her face. "Everything's set up the way you like it. The team is doing tests on the soil and the structure so we know what we're up against."

I nod. "Great. Anything in particular I need to be aware of before we get going?"

Her smile falters. That's not good. It normally means someone is trying to make our lives difficult. I hate it when they do that.

"There's someone waiting for you in the main tent. He says his name is Sawyer..."

I groan.

"Do you know him?"

"We've crossed paths."

Angelica raises an eyebrow. "That bad?"

"You don't know the half of it."

A part of me wishes I'd stayed in Egypt rather than coming back to my home country, especially if I have to deal with Sawyer Tarly. His reputation is well known throughout the archaeology world. And that's without adding my personal experiences of him into the mix.

And how much he hates me.

"I'll deal with him, just make sure everyone is ready for when the testing teams have finished. Do they have an estimate for when that'll be?"

"They're hoping tomorrow, but it might be the day after."

"Okay. Great. If that's the case, I'll deal with Mr Tarly and do a tour of the area, and then I'll be going on a personal errand."

Angelica's eyebrows shoot up.

"I live not far from here," I say by way of an explanation. Though I suppose technically, that's not *really* true. My official and legal accommodation is about an hour away, but I spend most of my life jumping between dig sites and living in tents. I wouldn't want it any other way, but I'm looking forward to seeing my best friend again, it's been too long since I spent an evening hanging out with Willow.

"Will you still be reachable?" Angelica asks.

"Of course." I may want to spend some time doing personal stuff, but that doesn't mean I've forgotten I'm in charge of this dig. I refuse to leave my team in the lurch. Most of them will already know that. Even if we're halfway around the world from normal, most of them agreed to come with me.

"Excellent. Where am I to tell people you are if they ask?" Angelica asks.

"Just off-site will do." Anything more than that and people might start talking about where they think I am. The last thing I want is for them to turn up at my best friend's coffee shop and overwhelm her right around the time I want to spend time with her. After I've gone is fine, that'll be good for her business and she makes the best coffee.

Angelica nods and makes a note on her clipboard. "I'll send you the end of the day summary as normal."

"Thanks. I'll go deal with Mr Tarly now. Hopefully, he won't be much of a problem going forward that way." Knowing Sawyer, that might not be an option.

"Got it." She waves and heads over to one of the supervisors running the tests.

I sigh. I wish we could get some of it done quicker, but there are only so many tests we can do on-site, most have to be sent off to a proper lab before we can do anything else.

But that's okay. I'm used to this part. It's often weeks until we can get a dig started, but this one is relatively small so it shouldn't take as long.

Depending on what Sawyer wants.

I take the long route to the main tent, trying to formulate some kind of plan about what to say to him. I never expected to see him again after we broke up, despite working in similar fields. But he's always focused on the British history side of things, while I've spent most of my career in Africa and the Middle East.

Putting thousands of miles between the two of us meant I never really had to deal with the fallout of our relationship. He wasn't wrong when he accused me of running away from what was between us. I've never truly gotten over him, which is making me even less confident about going in to see him.

But there's only so long I can put it off without raising suspicions, and I need to clear the way for my team to do their jobs.

This is not how I wanted to start my dig.

2

THE MOMENT I enter the main tent, I know I'm in trouble.

Sawyer's back is turned to me, but I don't need to see his front to know he's been working out a lot since I last saw him. The muscles on his back ripple as he moves, even under his shirt.

My mouth runs dry.

This does not bode well for me, and I don't even know *what* he wants yet.

I clear my throat. "Mr Tarly, to what do I owe this pleasure?"

He spins around, his eyes widening in surprise as he takes me in.

"Sabine? What are you doing here?" He drags his gaze up and down me.

Suddenly I'm regretting the practical clothing and lack of makeup I picked this morning, even though I know it's best for the environment I'm in.

"You asked to see the person in charge of the dig," I say, my voice not even wavering slightly. That's a relief, I thought I was going to be a complete and utter mess.

"You're in charge?"

"You don't need to sound so surprised." I cross my arms across my chest and try to look unimpressed.

"I didn't think you did digs around here."

"I don't normally, but I was asked to supervise this one personally."

"Ah."

"That doesn't explain why you're here," I point out. "I pick each and every member of my team myself, unless you've lied on an application form, your name isn't on that list."

"It isn't," he agrees.

"So, what are you doing here?" I'm not sure whether to be saddened or relieved that it isn't to do with me, but he didn't seem like he was expecting me to enter the tent, which I suspect rules out some scenarios.

"I'm from the Department of Magical Heritage."

I raise an eyebrow. "If I remember correctly, you didn't see eye to eye with them."

"They funded my Master's Degree after you left," he responds stiffly.

I try to ignore the slight heat which rises to my cheeks. I didn't leave to get away with him, I was offered an apprenticeship that I couldn't turn down. And I'm grateful for it every day considering that's how I got to where I am now.

"What does the DMH want with our little dig?"

"They want you to put a stop to it."

I close my eyes and take a deep breath. "They've already approved the dig. I wouldn't be here if they hadn't." I saw nothing in the permit paperwork that even suggested there was any controversy over this.

"There's been some miscommunication between the departments," Sawyer says.

"Right. So what you're saying is that the excavation has been approved, is still approved, but someone who didn't check all the details before the paperwork was completed and sent back to me, doesn't want this to happen for one reason or another?"

He purses his lips, clearly unhappy with my statement but unable to refute it.

"Am I wrong?" I prompt once it's clear he isn't going to say anything.

"No, you're not."

"Then I fail to see why this warrants a personal visit."

"I'm here to urge you to stop the dig and consider the dangers."

"It's a stone, Sawyer. It's less dangerous than most of what I deal with."

"That's what you think," he mutters darkly.

I resist the urge to roll my eyes. "I'm guessing you have inconclusive research for me to read so I can make up my own mind?"

He glares at me, clearly unimpressed by my accurate observation. While I haven't had to deal with him in this context before, I have had to deal with plenty of other condescending warlocks who assume I don't *understand* that investigating ancient sites can come with dangers.

It's like they don't think there's a reason for the curse breakers who are part of our dig teams when it comes to magical sites. Though admittedly, the curse breaker I *want* is too busy with her final exams at Grimalkin Academy to be onsite right now. She's promised that if I need her, then I can call her and she'll come. I hope that won't be necessary. While she's well aware that she has a job offer when she leaves regardless of what her marks are like, I know she'll want the security of decent grades.

"It's not inconclusive," Sawyer says with the hint of a huff. "It's said that the Humber Stone is the gateway to hell..."

"It's also said that it's just a stone," I point out. "I can't make my decisions based on what it *might* be when that's precisely what I'm being paid to find out."

"Sabine, please." There's almost a begging note in his voice. "At least look at the information before doing this."

I sigh. He has a point. If I don't look at what he's brought and then one of my team member's gets hurt, I'm never going to forgive myself.

"Fine. Let me see."

He gestures to the low table in front of him which is covered in various pieces of paper. I'd thought they were related to the general organisation of the dig, but it turns out I'm wrong.

"I see you made yourself at home."

"If you said no, I was going to clear it up really slowly and hope you got frustrated enough that you came to help and then saw something that interested you," he admits.

"Ah, that trick." He'd used it on me a few times while we'd still been at the academy together.

It had worked every time. I'm sure it would have done this one too. A lot had changed in the time we'd spent apart, but not *that* much.

I step up to the table and start scanning the pages he's laid out.

"This one is of particular interest," he says, pointing to a photocopy of an old scroll.

I lean over and peer at it, trying not to let myself get distracted by his familiar scent.

Bits and pieces of the research catch my attention, but none of the sources he's brought seem to agree on one very important thing.

What the Humber Stone is.

"This is only supporting the need for this excavation," I point out. "If no one has any idea what the stone is, then we need to find out."

"Or we could just leave it alone and not invoke something ancient and vengeful."

I raise an eyebrow. "Do you really think that's going to happen?"

"Maybe I've seen one too many horror films, but I don't want to tempt fate. Do you?"

I groan. Is he seriously still obsessed with those things? "Why do you still watch them if they make you paranoid?"

"Because I enjoy them and they teach me the proper amount of caution. Maybe they should have made you watch more while you were doing your apprenticeship."

"I had lots of other things to focus on."

"Like dead bodies?"

"Don't talk about that here," I mutter.

"You haven't told anyone that you're a necromancer, have you?"

I sigh. "It's not an easy thing to bring up. Most people get so squeamish about it as if they think I'm going to kill them in their sleep. You know it doesn't work like that."

"Maybe if you trusted them with the information, they'd surprise you. And you could help remove some of the stigma."

"Perhaps. But I don't trust people. Though I suspect most of them know anyway."

"How?"

"There's a lot of smart people on this team. I'm sure more than one of them has figured out I'm stronger magically when we find a large cache of well-preserved bodies, it doesn't take a genius to figure it out."

No matter how hard I try to hide it, some things are just unavoidable. That's one of them. I can't control when my magic recharges, nor would I want to. Getting a magic boost from the ancient dead is something most necromancers can only dream of. Most of my kind spend their lives living next to graveyards and pretending to be witches. Funnily enough, that was how I'd ended up at Grimalkin Academy and meeting Sawyer in the first place.

"Then you should tell them. You could end up losing some of their loyalty if they work it out and you haven't been honest with them."

I purse my lips, not wanting to admit that it's something I've been worrying about since the beginning.

"I think you should stop sticking your nose in where it shouldn't be," I snap.

Surprise flits through his eyes. I don't think he expected me to be so sharp with him. And he has a point. No matter what my personal feelings are, Sawyer is here in a professional capacity and as am I. That means I need to act like it. Especially as the DMH not only controls many of the places of interest in this country, but have far-reaching connections in other countries around the world too. The last thing I need is for him to make a report that harms my reputation and then I end up banned from making any kind of contributions in my own field.

"How long are you planning on observing the dig for?" I ask instead.

"Until you stop it."

"Right. So you should plan for at least three weeks."

"If that's how long it's going to be, then I am."

I scowl. Somehow, I thought he'd be easier to put off than this.

"Well, if that's everything, I'm afraid I need to get going. I have an appointment to keep..."

"You mean you're going to see Willow."

"It's none of your business where I go," I counter. "If you need anything, Angelica is around." Though I'll be telling her to keep a close eye on him, the last thing I want is to leave him running around my dig site and doing untold damage.

I don't wait for him to respond and walk out of the tent, my whole body on edge from the encounter.

Going to see Willow is *just* what I need right now. Time away from the intensity of the dig.

And from Sawyer. I may not have been around

him for long, but it's enough to have put me on edge. And to remind me of everything I lost when we broke up. Having him around is going to be dangerous for me, I can tell.

THE BELL above the door tinkles as I push through it and get hit with the heavy scent of roasted coffee beans. I close my eyes and take a deep breath. I may not spend much time here, but this is my home.

"Sabine!"

Before I've even fully registered my name, my best friend throws her arms around me and hugs me tightly.

"I wasn't expecting you until the weekend," Willow says as she pulls back to look at me. "Did you need something?"

I chuckle slightly uncomfortably. "If I say yes, is that bad?"

She shakes her head in bemusement. "I'd expect

nothing less. But you'll have to pay the toll if you want help."

"Oh? And what is that?"

"You can tell me about the teapot," she says, gesturing to the antique pot sitting on the side.

I know it well. The witch I want to make into my curse breaker and her boyfriend found it as part of the huge discovery they made in Egypt. It was an enigma to everyone on the dig and it was a relief when it disappeared. At least, it was for everyone else. It wasn't for me when I realised it was in my tent. Nor when I boxed it up without realising it and wrote the address for my best friend's coffee shop on the label. I'm still not sure what compelled me to do it. There's something about the pot that I can't explain. And I don't like that. I'm used to being able to work out the secrets of objects. It's literally my job.

"I don't have any explanation," I admit. "It's almost like it made me do things."

She eyes the pot warily, then nods. "I get that. It makes me take it upstairs with me at the end of the day." Something odd passes over her face. "I think it's alive."

Alarm floods through me. What if it's sucking the life force out of her or something like that? I had all of the curse detectors on the team look over it several times and they didn't find anything, but we don't know all the kinds of magic the ancient witches and warlocks had at their disposal. And it's not a necromancer object, I'd have figured that out instantly.

"And how are you feeling? You're not extra tired? Hungrier than normal? Craving something you don't normally..."

"Sabine," she cuts me off sharply. "I'm fine. You don't have to worry about me."

"But the teapot..."

"Is friendly."

I raise an eyebrow, but don't argue with her. Willow is a good judge of character, if she thinks the teapot isn't going to hurt her, then it probably isn't.

She heads behind the counter and starts pulling out the various ingredients to make me a coffee. Affection towards her floods through me. She's one of the reasons I agreed to this dig. We message all the time, but that doesn't mean I don't miss her.

"You're looking well. Did you manage to recharge on a pile of old bones or something?" Willow asks as she slides an iced coffee across the counter to me.

"Thanks," I say as I take it. "And it was a mummy, you know bones don't do much."

She gives an exaggerated shiver. "It's weird that's what you do."

"I don't have any control over how I have to recharge my magic," I point out. "I'm not like you with an endless supply fuelled by nothing. I have to be around death. This is just less creepy than hanging around a hospital."

"You're not wrong there," she mutters. "Though I still haven't *seen* any necromancers doing that."

"How much time are you spending at the hospital?"

"Barely any, especially since I broke it off with the doctor."

A rattle comes from the direction of the teapot, drawing our attention to it.

"Does it do that often?" I ask.

Willow shrugs. "Sometimes, I think it's jealous."

"How can a teapot be jealous?"

"How can a lot of things be the case," she counters. "It just is."

"I can find someone to take it off you if you want..."

"No need. I like the company. I know that sounds weird."

"I've known you were weird for at least ten years," I point out.

"True. And now you're stuck with me. They say if a friendship lasts seven years then it's going to be for life," she says brightly. "Are you staying here every night?"

I nod. "The dig is only about an hour away."

"I know, I checked it on the map. It's nice for you to be so close to home for a change. How was the site?"

"About what you'd expect, it's a big green field with a stone in the middle of it."

"That sounds riveting," she quips as she makes her way around from the counter and comes to sit in one of the comfy chairs next to me.

"Mmmhmm." I drink some of my coffee. It's delicious, but no surprise there. She wouldn't be running a coffee shop as successfully as this one if it wasn't.

"I found a product online that might appeal to any necromancer customers I might get. Do you mind if I order some and test it on you?"

I glance around the coffee shop to check for other patrons, relieved to find it empty, but not surprised. Willow wouldn't out my species in front of other people.

"I can, but I don't think they'll be ordering it." I

can't see any necromancers outing themselves by ordering coffee any time soon.

She shakes her head. "I wouldn't have them order a coffee with death or anything obvious like that. They'd come and ask me for my famous spiderweb latte."

"Please tell me it doesn't include actual spiders." I shudder dramatically.

"For someone who spends a lot of time in old abandoned buildings, it's surprising you hate spiders as much as you do."

"I can't help it." Though she does have a point. If I'm honest with myself, I thought I'd be over it by now too.

"There are no spiders," she promises.

"Then I'll try it, but I can't promise anything about necromancers coming in." I take a sip of my coffee. Now she's talking about it, a shot of something to perk up my necromancy wouldn't be completely amiss.

She shrugs. "That's fine. I just don't want them thinking I'm excluding them. I want everyone to know they're welcome here."

A genuine smile spreads over my face. If there's anyone I believe that of, it's Willow. She wants everyone to be happy, especially her clientele.

"So, you were telling me about the dig site," she prompts.

"Oh, right. The most interesting thing is probably that Sawyer was there."

"What?" Her voice almost breaks it goes that high. "You talked about spiders and didn't lead with that? What was he doing there? *Please* tell me he was there to beg for you back?"

I chuckle. I'm sure it's been a secret fantasy of hers that we'd get back together. She loves a good romantic story. "Not even slightly. He was there for the Department of Magical Heritage."

"Oh eesh, that's not good."

"It's not bad either. He wants me to stop the excavation, but the DMH has already approved it."

"That sounds like quite the quandary."

"For him, yes. For me, not so much. My dig will continue as planned."

"Is he going to keep hanging around?" she asks.

I shrug. "No idea."

"Just...be careful if he does."

My eyebrows shoot up. I thought she liked the idea of the two of us getting back together. She did always like Sawyer.

"Don't look at me like that," she says, correctly

interpreting my look. "I want whatever you want for yourself. That's my job as best friend."

"Hmm."

"I liked Sawyer, and he was good for you while you were together. But if he's not good for you now, then I don't support it."

"Thanks, Willow." Truth be told, I'm not really sure *what* I want from Sawyer. Neither of us were fully at fault for our relationship ending, but that doesn't mean it didn't hurt.

"Just trust yourself. Your heart will lead you in the right direction," she promises.

"I hope you're right."

"I normally am."

I shake my head in bemusement, somewhat refreshed from being back in her presence.

My phone vibrates from its place in my pocket. I groan. Only one number is set to do that right now, and it's not good news.

I pull it out and check the screen.

Six missed calls, all from Angelica. That's *not* a good sign.

"Bad news?" Willow asks.

"They need me back at the dig site."

"But you'll be home tonight, right?"

I nod.

"Great, I'll have your bed made up for you." Which sounds like a lot of work, but I know her, she'll just flick her wand and it'll all be done in no time.

"Thanks." I down the rest of my iced coffee, half tempted to ask her for the road. But I don't. If there's anything about excavation sites that I don't like, it's the facilities. I'd much rather use a proper bathroom, which means not overloading myself with coffee.

"I'll see you in a bit," Willow calls as I'm heading out of the room.

"Bye!" I shout back, grateful that she's understanding about me disappearing after only a couple of hours. I suppose she's more likely than anyone to understand, she's currently at work too.

I'll be back before I know it. And hopefully, I'll have a couple of days at the end of my stay where I can help her around the coffee shop and spend some time with her.

Fingers crossed nothing goes wrong to stop that.

I PARK BADLY next to a pick-up truck. I have no idea which team member it belongs to. Probably none of them. We often drive rentals, but as this is home for most of us, some are driving family cars. I jump out and rush over to the tent where they're supposed to be processing the soil samples we can do on-site. A lot of them have to be sent off in order to be properly tested, but we like to get preliminary results so we know what to expect.

People are running around in a not-very-orderly fashion. A frown pulls at my features. This isn't how a dig is supposed to be. I train my team well, and they know better than to rush. That's how mistakes are made.

I push through the tent flap and enter an even more hectic environment.

"What's going on?" I ask Lenny as he passes me.

The pedologist pushes his glasses up his nose, a nervous tick and the only time he actually seems to touch them.

"The machines are broken," he admits. "Or we think they are. I'm not sure."

"How can you not be sure?" I try to remain calm. Broken soil testing machines are frustrating, but not the end of the world.

He titters nervously. "They seem to act normally when we use the control samples, but whenever we try to process something that's come from around the stone..."

My heart sinks. Is this seriously happening?

I glance across the room to spot Sawyer standing with his arms crossed and a smug expression on his face. Almost like this is what he expected to happen.

I resist the urge to flip him the finger. Or worse, stick my tongue out at him. But I can't act so immaturely around my team, I'll never manage to keep their respect if I do, especially being a woman. While a lot of people don't care, there are some that do, and I don't want to give them any excuses to take my projects away from me.

"What about the labs? Surely they're having better luck."

"The samples we sent today are just arriving, but we got some earlier in the week that they've processed already." He pauses, as if trying to search for the right words to say whatever bad news is coming next. "Kind of."

I sigh. "What do you mean, *kind of*?"

"I think you'd better talk to them yourself." He gestures to the computer station at the back of the tent, which isn't as fancy as it sounds. It's just a laptop hooked up to the generator we use to run all of the electronic equipment and the hotspot we create for the wifi.

I make my way over to it. "Are they expecting my call?"

Lenny nods. "They asked us to get you as soon as you got here."

"Good. Let's get this over with." I shake the mouse and wake up the screen. A blue phone sits in the middle of the screen with a video icon next to it. They've got everything set up and waiting for me. I like that, even if I have a bad feeling about the situation.

"Do you mind if I sit in?" Sawyer asks.

I jump ever so slightly, surprised to find him so

close to me. "Sure, if you want."

I don't know what's keeping him here, but knowing Sawyer it'll be some kind of professional curiosity. Or maybe he wants to write a paper on the Humber Stone. It's been a while since he published anything new.

Embarrassment sweeps through me as I realise what it means for me to have been keeping up with his career. I like to tell myself that it's normal to check up on my ex like that, but I don't think it is.

I suppose I can try and pretend it's professional. While his job at the DMH isn't what I'd call my thing, a lot of his research into sites of magical interest around the world does fall inside my job parameters. Knowing what's going on with a cave in Brazil could help me with my excavation of a cave in France.

In theory.

I'm well aware that's not the *real* reason I keep an eye on his publications.

I push the thoughts aside. Right now, I need to focus on the call I'm about to make and finding out what's happening with the soil. I hit the call button and wait for it to connect.

The picture blinks into life, revealing a gorgeous

woman with curly hair and a complexion that I would kill for. Maybe.

"Hi, you must be Sabine," she says. "I'm Drea, I'm in charge of the team testing your soil samples."

"It's nice to meet you," I respond. "I'm sure you know Lenny already. This is Sawyer Tarly, he's from the Department of Magical Heritage."

"I didn't realise they were funding the excavation."

"They aren't," I say firmly. "Mr Tarly has a professional interest in the site. He's here for that reason only."

From the picture on the screen, it almost appears as if he's going to argue with that, but thinks better of it.

Good. I don't care why he's still hanging around all the time. It's a free country and he can do whatever he wants to. But if he interferes with my work, I'll be the one to kick him off the site myself.

Though now I think about it, I'm not sure I *want* him to be gone. As annoying as I find it when he's looking as smug as he is right now, there's no doubt I've been looking forward to seeing him again since parting the first time.

"Lenny suggested there's a problem with the soil samples?" I ask Drea.

She nods. "Was any magic used in recovering them?"

I glance at Lenny, reasonably sure the answer is no, especially as that's what I specified, but I want to make sure.

"None at all," he confirms. "They've been taken using the same kits we'd use on a non-magical site so that the soil can be tested properly."

"I thought as much. There's something strange about them, though," Drea continues.

"Strange how?"

"They're not reading properly on any of our equipment. We can make some educated guesses on the samples based on the appearance and texture, but there's nothing more we can do. Only the samples from a mile away from the site are behaving normally."

I close my eyes and count to ten, trying to centre myself and not lose patience with the entire dig site. It isn't Drea's fault the soil is being funny, nor is it Lenny's so long as the team has done everything by the book. And I'm sure they have. He's not the kind of person to skip a step for any reason.

"We've taken a new set of samples," Lenny says, proving my thoughts to be correct. "Someone should be with you in the next hour or so with them."

"Thanks. I'll have the team on standby so we can have someone test them straight away, but I'm not convinced we're going to get different results this time," she admits.

"Me neither," Lenny agrees. "The samples aren't behaving any differently on this end either."

"Would you mind copying me in on the email when you send the results over?" I ask. Normally, Lenny just gives me a rundown of everything once it's done. He'll happily show me charts and reports for days, if I let him, but I honestly don't understand most of it. I've tried to read books to at least understand the basics, but it's just one of those things I don't understand no matter what I do.

"Of course. I'll include a summary in layman's terms, if you'd like?" she suggests.

"That would be good." I don't want to admit to this woman that I have no idea what half the words mean, but that doesn't mean I won't accept a simpler explanation now she's offering one.

"Okay, I'll see to that. It was good to speak with you," she says.

"You too."

We end the call and I turn away, trying to contain my frustration.

"What do you want us to do?" Lenny asks.

"Keep testing," I respond. "Until you think there's no point. I'll leave that to your discretion. We can't advance without this information, and if that's the case, then I'll deal with it."

Please don't let that be the case. I don't want Sawyer to be right. And not just because he'll be really smug about it. I also don't want this dig to be a failure. It means a lot to me that I was asked to be the team leader instead of having to bid for it like normal. If I mess it up...

I push the thought to the side. These things happen all the time. My career is going to be just fine if I don't have a successful dig.

But that's not the point.

5

I POUR over the various reports and photos in front of me, trying to make sense of what I'm seeing. This excavation is supposed to have been an easy one. Something I could do in a couple of weeks while visiting my friends and family as well as looking good in my portfolio.

Though there's a little part of me that really is intrigued about the Humber Stone too. The fact that something can exist in one place for so long and nobody knows anything about it is amazing. Even the fae don't know if the report from one of the local courts is to be believed. Then again, when it comes to fae, anything is impossible. They might not like to lie, but they're capable of it, especially if they think it's important to keep something a secret. It's a loophole a lot of people don't know about, which only makes the fae more dangerous to be around and not less.

I pick up their report again and scan through it. Nothing sets me on edge. I don't think this is one of the cases where they're keeping a secret.

The tent flap rustles and Sawyer steps inside.

Instead of annoyance rushing through me, it's relief. While at first, I wasn't sure if I wanted him around, I'm starting to enjoy the fact he wants to spend time with me, especially at this dig.

"Is everything all right? You look annoyed," he asks.

I sigh. "I'm just trying to figure out what's going on." I wave the hand with the report in it around.

He reaches out and takes it from me. His eyebrows raise as he reads through it. "This isn't a report we've got at the DMH."

"Believe it or not, I did order a selection of my own," I deadpan.

"So I see. And you have a fae contact? I'm impressed. They like to keep to themselves."

"No, they don't like to lie about things and think it's easier if they don't put themselves in situations where they have to," I counter. "But as for how, one of the apprentices a few years back was a fae girl who didn't want to go down any of their traditional career paths. She went back to her court recently, but we've kept in contact for when she's ready to rejoin us on the team."

Surprise flits across his face, whether it's because I had a fae working for me in the first place, or because I keep in contact with ex-employees who I wouldn't mind working with again, I'm not sure.

"I asked her if she knew anything about it when I found out I was coming here and this is the report she sent me." I point to the piece of paper in his hand. "If I'm not mistaken, the fae seem as confused as everyone else about it."

"Who else do you have reports from?" he asks, setting the piece of paper down neatly.

"Nymphs, dryads, a local wolf shifter pack who never assimilated with the others, a long-dead druid, an expert warlock. Even a pixie and a mer. Absolutely no one knows about this stone."

"You have a lot of contacts."

"And you don't? What we do isn't that different," I point out.

"Not according to you."

I sigh. "It's not that I think the DMH isn't valuable work," I admit. "It's just that I remember you talking about all the adventures you wanted to have and the countries you wanted to explore."

"Ah, yes. I remember you being particularly fond of the idea of the waterfall in Peru."

"The pictures were beautiful," I say wistfully, trying not to think about the *other* part of the adventure he used to describe to me. "Did you ever go?"

"No."

"Why not?"

"I suppose the time was never right," he admits, but I can hear the reluctance in his voice. He knows I'm not going to buy it.

"Maybe you should think about that before it's too late to do anything about it anymore," I suggest.

He's about to respond when a series of shrieks outside draw our attention.

We exchange a worried glance even as I jump to my feet and we rush towards the tent exit.

Several people rush past us as we make our way outside.

I reach out to grab one of them. "What's going on?" I ask.

"The main tent's collapsed," she responds.

I blink a few times. "How?"

"No one knows. Angelica checked everything this morning like she normally does and everything was fine and in place. It just kind of..." She folds her hands in on one another to simulate a collapsing tent.

I close my eyes and take a deep breath.

"Is anyone hurt?" That's the most important question on my mind.

"I don't think so. As far as we know, no one was inside."

Phew. That's something, at least.

"All right, I'll go take a look. Has anything been damaged, do you know?"

"No idea, sorry." She heads on her way to help the rest of the team put the tent back to rights.

"How is this happening?" I mutter.

"It could be the stone?" Sawyer suggests.

I throw him a withering look. "It's a rock," I remind him.

"A *mysterious* rock." An impish smile flashes across his features, revealing his tease. Though that doesn't mean he believes the Humber Stone is innocent, he's just enjoying teasing me too much.

"Let's go check it out. If we can figure out how the rock did it, then maybe we can talk some sense into it."

He opens his mouth to argue but I hold my hand up to stop him.

"If a stone can be to blame for the tent collapsing, then talking to it shouldn't be a problem."

"You have a point."

"Does the DMH have any evidence of any other sentient rock?" I ask as we walk through the camp.

Most of the team already seems to be congregated around the main tent, which is good. The sooner I know the damage, the sooner I can make a judgement call on what to do.

"None that I know about, but it could just be that I've never come across one before. I can make a call and get one of my interns to do some digging, if you want?"

I nod, hardly believing I'm sanctioning this course of investigation. But one of the reasons they wanted me to head up this excavation in the first place is because I like to leave no stone unturned. A small wave of amusement travels through me at my own pun. It's a shame no one else can appreciate it. If there's something in another case or situation that can help me uncover the truth about the Humber Stone, then I need to know it. Maybe it'll even hold the answers to how to deal with it.

Because we're clearly not going about this the

right way. And something has to change before my entire camp ends up struck by lightning or taken out by an earthquake.

It seems I'm starting to believe in Sawyer's theories about the stone after all. *Just* what I need.

6

THE SKY IS CLEARER than it normally is at this time of year, with the twinkling stars and bright moonlight showing me the way through the camp and towards the Humber Stone without the need for any torchlight. It gives the atmosphere a kind of mythical feel, especially with how quiet it is now all the other members of the excavation team have gone home. There are some security guards off in the distance, but they won't disturb me. They probably don't even know I'm here, which doesn't say much about their skills as guards, but they're mostly a deterrent anyway.

The stone sits in the same place it always has, with only a small portion of it poking up above the ground. Or what we all assume is only a small part of it. For all we know, this is the complete stone. But that doesn't *feel* right. Something about it says that it used to be grand.

I sit myself down on the grass beside it and stare at the rough surface. Speckles of moss mar the weathered surface, just like I'd expect there to be given the stone's age and location. Nothing about the appearance of the Humber Stone suggests it's as special as it is. The uniqueness is all part of its mystery. No one knows why it's here or what it's supposed to be for, and that gives it power.

I close my eyes and soak in the air around me. It isn't imbued with the power of the dead, which suggests that it's not a tombstone of some kind. I never really thought it was. That's one of the few things there aren't rumours about. But it's an easy thing for me to check.

"What are you?" I murmur, not having the confidence to talk to the stone at full volume. I feel crazy doing this. I think it would be easier if it had a face of some kind, even one of the Green Men faces people like to carve on buildings around the country. They've always felt powerful to me, even if they're only depictions of an ethereal being that's no longer part of the world as far as anyone knows.

Unsurprisingly, the stone doesn't answer. I don't know how I expected it to. Maybe telepathically?

I sigh. "Is it you that's trying to disrupt the camp?" I ask. "I'd really like it if you stopped. You're causing a lot of problems."

If an accusation isn't going to rouse it, then I don't know what will.

"I promise we're not here to hurt you. We just want to find out what you are. When we're done, you'll still be here and in one piece, we'll just know how better to take care of you," I promise.

I feel like a fool. I've been in all kinds of places, and seen altars and places of worship aplenty, but this stone is the first excavation subject I've ever talked to like this.

A scuffle sounds behind me and I glance up, only partly surprised to find Sawyer approaching with a small hamper in his left hand.

"I thought I'd find you here." He sits down next to me without waiting for me to invite him too. He's probably guessed I won't mind the company.

I nod. I'm not surprised he worked it out, I did mention talking to the stone.

He flips open the hamper and pulls out a bottle of amber liquid. "You still like mead, right?"

"Yes. But I'm at work."

"No, you're at your place of work talking to a stone," he reminds me. "Technically, you're not on the clock."

He has a point. Maybe drinking some will make the conversation go more smoothly. "I can put it away if you want," he says.

"No need. You're right."

He nods and pulls out three small drams. He fills them quickly and hands one to me before getting to his feet and picking up the second one. He closes the small distance to the stone and pours it out at the foot of it.

The amber liquid disappears among the grass, almost as if the soil is drinking it up.

Sawyer shrugs as he heads back to me. "If the stone is sentient, then it feels rude not to offer it some of what we're drinking."

"Just be careful not to give it too much, we've seen the damage it can inflict sober, imagine what will happen if we have a sentient *drunk* rock on our hands."

A loud snort slips from Sawyer. "I dread to think."

He picks up his own dram and holds it out to me. I clink mine against his, staring straight into his eyes. It's bad luck to look away while making a toast.

"Cheers," I whisper.

"Cheers," he replies, holding my gaze.

Neither of us move, frozen in time. Or maybe between time. I'm not too sure which. Something lies heavily in the air between us, reminding me of the days and nights we spent with one another when we were in our early twenties. Other than Willow, he'd been my whole world. Someone who finally believed that being a necromancer didn't mean I had to spend my entire life hidden away and could never make a name for myself. I guess he was right about that after all, I'm doing just fine for myself despite my species being the most hunted in the world. Technically, the necromancer hunts were supposed to have stopped, but the vampires are still scared of us, even the born ones who wouldn't charge our magic unless they were proper-dead. I suppose the turned vampires may have a point. They died as whatever they were before they turned into a vampire, and can be a good source of power for a necromancer if they have no morals. What most of the people hunting us seemed to lack comprehension of is that most necromancers don't *want* to hurt anyone.

I pull myself out of my thoughts and down my dram of mead. The sweet taste explodes on my tongue and the alcohol warms my insides.

"This is good stuff," I say, breaking the growing silence between us.

The silence that's trying to tell us something.

"Someone at work makes it according to a traditional recipe. It's pricey, but worth it."

"It really is. Does he sell it? I might need to stock up on it to celebrate all of my triumphs with."

He chuckles. "He does. I'll send you the website later."

"Thanks."

We lapse into silence, a surprisingly comfortable one given everything that's ever been between us. I try not to dwell on that. How much I like Sawyer is definitely a problem in managing to keep myself from doing anything stupid.

I sigh.

"A penny for your thoughts?" he asks.

I shrug. "Nothing special. I'm just wondering about the rock and how I'm going to find out the truth about it. It just doesn't make any sense."

"Maybe it's not meant to?" he suggests.

"Hang on..."

He cocks his head to the side and waits for me to continue, a familiar gesture I've always loved.

"Do you have an actual penny?"

"No. But I can sort that out." He pulls out his wand and flicks it, calling up his magic with ease. A glittering penny falls to the ground beneath the point of his wand.

"I thought you couldn't conjure money?" I spent enough time at the academy surrounded by witches and warlocks to know how annoyed they all got about that.

"I can't. But I have a bowl at home I can summon it from. It's saved me a few times when I need to pay for parking."

"Smart."

"I thought so." He holds the coin out to me.

I take it gingerly, trying to stop our hands from touching so I don't get too consumed by him.

"What are you going to do with it?" he asks.

"Maybe the stone is some kind of wishing well type thing." I hold the coin out and close my eyes. "I wish we can uncover the secrets of the Humber Stone." I flick it off my hand and towards the stone.

Within seconds, it's hurtling back towards me and strikes me on the cheek.

"Ouch." I wince and rub my face where the penny hit. It hurts a surprising amount.

Sawyer tries to smother a laugh, but doesn't manage very well.

I glare at him. "Maybe it's cursed after all," I mutter.

"A curse is easy to deal with," he points out. "It's some of the other options you have to worry about."

"*Curses*," I whisper and jump to my feet.

"Sabine? What's happening?"

"I know just who to call." I'm already heading back in the direction of my car, determined to get the one witch I know with the capability to break a curse this strong on the phone.

THE TENT FLAP lifts up and the young witch I've called to help slips in. She doesn't look like she's just come out of an exam, but that's what she said she was doing this morning, and I don't think she'd lie about it.

"Sorry, traffic," she says as she sets down her bag. "What am I looking at?" She glances around the room, trying to find the object I was her to break the curse on.

She has no idea what's in store for her.

Her gaze lands on Sawyer and surprise flits across her face.

"You're Sawyer Tarly," she says.

"I am," he agrees.

"I read a lot of your papers while I was writing

my dissertation. Your grasp on magical sites is unparalleled."

"Oh, er, thank you." He's visibly uncomfortable by her praise.

"Sawyer, this is Monica Black, she's my soon-to-be curse breaker. Once she's finished studying at Grimalkin."

"Everyone calls me Mona," she adds cheerily.

He raises an eyebrow. "A student?"

"For now," she agrees. "But I'll be graduating soon."

"Mona is one of the most talented curse breakers I've ever worked with," I assure him. "I've never met anyone who could pull off the feats she does."

A blush rises to her cheeks. "I'm not *that* good."

"What's the most difficult curse you've broken?" Sawyer asks, clearly intrigued. He's known me long enough to know I'm not going to lie about anything like this. I want the best teams around me, I don't care about age or where they came from, if they're at the top of their field, I want them for my team.

"I broke a curse on myself a few years ago," she admits sheepishly. "I couldn't cast a spell without conjuring a kitten."

"Please tell me you didn't bring any of them with you today?" I ask, remembering the havoc one of them caused at the last dig of mine she attended. The kitten had also managed to find a huge treasure haul unlike any from the past five years and had cemented all of our names in the history books, but that wasn't the point.

She laughs uneasily. "I checked my bag six times and had my friend count them once I left. All eleven are accounted for back at the academy," she assures me.

I nod. "Good. But what she's not telling you is that there wasn't a counterspell for her curse. She had to make one."

Disbelief shines through Sawyer's eyes. "You *made* a counter curse?"

"Yes. Though not on my own. My best friend helped."

"And is she a fifty-year-old witch who has been working on counter curses her entire life?" Sawyer asks.

"No, she's twenty-one too."

"Fascinating."

"We're hoping to get on the honour roll at the academy for our counter curse work."

"You're more likely to get a Nobel Prize for something like that," he mutters.

"I don't need anything like that. I just wanted to

stop making kittens all the time and actually be able to do magic properly. Now I can." She shrugs. "So, what am I supposed to be breaking a curse on?"

"Come with me, I'll show you," I instruct, leading her out of the tent.

We make the short trip to where the top of the stone peeks out from the ground. We still haven't been able to dig around it to see how far down it goes. Every time we try, something breaks. First, it was the digger, then it was the spades. Nothing we do is working.

Mona frowns, studying it intently. "Ah."

"Can you feel a curse?"

She shakes her head. "But that doesn't mean there isn't one. Do you mind if I take a look?"

I shake my head. "Take as long as you want."

I watch with vague interest as she makes her way down to the stone and starts doing various tests on it.

"She broke a curse on herself? Really?" Sawyer asks once she's out of earshot.

"Yes. There are enough witness statements about it that it's to be believed. She protected herself and one of her boyfriends from a cave-in while in Egypt too. And that's without taking into account that she's powerful enough to create *living creatures* without even meaning to."

"That's a lot of talent," he muses.

I turn to face him, a stern expression on my face. "Don't you *dare* think of trying to poach her for the Department of Magical Heritage. I'm not losing someone this valuable to my team."

"Whoa." He holds his hands up to punctuate the word. "I'm not in charge of hiring anyway."

"That's not a no," I mutter.

"I don't want to steal a member of your team from you," he says firmly. "Now if *you* want to work at the DMH, then I'm sure I can put in a good word with Stephanie in Human Resources."

"I don't want to work for them, you know that. It's all desk work and boring forms."

"I'm here, aren't I?"

"And how often do you go out in the field, Sawyer? Hmm? You used to talk all the time about the amazing discoveries you wanted to make and the things you wanted to learn about the world. How much of that do you actually do?"

He glances away, unable to answer my question without proving my point.

"Exactly. I don't want that. I want adventure and excitement. I want to step onto a site without any answers and come away with some of them, and a lot more questions. You know that. It's why I made the decision I did."

He sighs. "Do you ever regret it?"

"Yes and no," the answer slips out of me before I have a chance to think about it. "I don't regret taking the apprenticeship itself. It gave me an amazing opportunity."

"Like the one you're giving her?" he asks, nodding towards Mona.

"Yes. Though I'm jumping straight to an actual job for her. I don't want to risk her getting a better offer."

Watching the young witch work only makes that decision even stronger. She's good at what she does, and has a passion for it. Those things don't often come along in someone so young, and she's only going to get better with experience.

"So what do you regret about the decision?"

"Us," I admit softly. "I didn't like the way we ended things." And I didn't like the way I missed him after, but it's probably best if I don't mention that part.

"I didn't either," he admits. "I thought about it a lot."

"It makes sense. We spent so much time together."

"Is there anyone now?" he asks. "A Mr Sabine?"

I snort. "No. What about you?"

"Not at the moment." He gives me a funny look that I can't put a name to.

I'm saved from having to work out what's going on between us by Mona approaching, a crestfallen expression on her face.

This isn't going to be good news.

"I don't know what's going on with that stone, but there's no curse for me to break. Something isn't right about it, though." She glances over her shoulder and then shivers.

"But it isn't a curse?" I check.

"Not one of the kind I've ever encountered. And it doesn't feel like it's witch made."

"Could it be something else?" Sawyer asks. "Necromancer perhaps."

I wince at the word, even though it's not about me.

Mona's gaze flickers to me so quickly, I almost don't notice.

Great. Even the interns have heard what I am, then. Sawyer may have a point about outright telling people the truth about me. Or maybe it's better if I just act as if everyone already knows and then don't care.

I'm not sure, I'll think about it later.

"I haven't encountered every type of curse around," Mona says. "But it's nothing I do recognise. And it doesn't feel like anyone I've met."

Sawyer nods.

"Thank you for trying anyway, I'm sorry for taking you away from your exams," I say.

Mona shrugs. "It's fine, I was ready for a break anyway. It's probably been good to me."

"I'll get Angelica to add the hours to payroll."

Her cheeks flush. "You don't have to do that," she murmurs.

"Of course I do. If you do work for me, you get paid. That's how it works. I don't care if it was just a few hours out of your day, or if you don't have all your qualifications yet, that's how it is."

"But I didn't do a good job," she protests.

"Did you try everything you safely could on the stone?"

"Of course."

"Then you did a great job. You won't always succeed at breaking a curse, but that doesn't mean you haven't done your job. If we could easily break everything we came across, we wouldn't need people like you who specialise in *finding* the answers."

She bites her bottom lip, clearly not at peace with the concept yet. That's fine, it'll come with time.

"Thank you, Sabine."

"You're welcome. Good luck with the rest of your exams."

"Thanks. It was good to meet you, Mr Tarly."

"Sawyer, please," he says.

She smiles and nods, almost skipping away.

"I think you might be her idol," I muse as we watch her retreat.

"Then you're clearly not paying any attention to the way she's looking at you," he observes. "Or the way she's paying attention to what you're saying."

"Hmm. Maybe."

"You should pay more attention to it too," he says. "There's good wisdom there."

I sigh. He may be right about that. Sometimes, I won't be able to find the answers, even if I want to.

I'm starting to be afraid that this is one of those times.

8

DESPITE THE SHINING SUN, the site is abandoned. There isn't even a rumble from the generator anymore. I close my eyes and try not to let it get to me. I've only called a halt to a dig once before, and that was because of an earthquake, not because of a cursed stone.

Not, not a cursed stone. Mona couldn't find even a hint of one on it. Which means my dig has been halted by *just* a stone.

I sigh, trying not to let it get to me.

"It might not be as bad as it seems," Sawyer says, coming up behind me and taking me by surprise.

"What are you doing here?" I ask. "Didn't you hear I called it off? You got what you wanted."

"Technically, my desires have nothing to do with

it," he points out. "I was here because my boss sent me, not because of any feelings I have about the Humber Stone."

I frown. Somehow, that distinction had escaped me until now.

"But my intern found something that might interest you," he says. "It's kind of curse breaking to the extreme. Far more advanced than anything your curse breaker could conjure, as powerful as she is." He holds out a sheet of paper to me.

I take it, intrigued but not hopeful.

My eyes widen as I scan the page. "I don't think *any* curse breaker would think of this."

"Not unless they happened to have a necromancer handy, no," he agrees. "But look at that, we have a necromancer, and a warlock, and no one around to see what we're up to."

"I'm not doing this kind of magic without at least one coffee."

"Then it's a good job I have one in my car waiting for you. Iced with a squirt of vanilla and a dollop of whipped cream, right?"

I blink a few times as I process the order he's parroting at me.

My order. One he hasn't heard me make for years.

"Yes, that's right."

"You wait here and I'll go get it," he says, already starting to walk away.

I want to ask why he didn't bring it with him in the first place, but there's no point. Maybe he thought it would distract me from the spell, or make me think he was here for the wrong reason.

No matter *why* he's done it, I'm just confused by the entire situation. What am I supposed to make of him buying me my coffee?

Sawyer is back within minutes and hands me the plastic takeaway cup. "I should have got one of those refillable ones."

Our fingers graze against one another as I take it from him, reminding me of the night before and how nice it had been to sit with him even if we had been talking to a stone at the time. I want more than that. One evening isn't enough. Neither is a week.

That's the thing with Sawyer, he's always so easy to be around. There was a time when I thought it would always be the two of us travelling around the world together. He'd do the research into whatever place our dig site was located, and I'd run the practical side of things. An unstoppable team solving the mysteries of history all around the globe.

I turn away from him lest he see the emotions clouding up my face. I've never regretted my choice to become an apprentice to the woman who started off my career, but right now I'm faced with the sadness of what I lost in the process and the sudden realisation that I've never dealt with it.

"Do you think we're capable of doing it?" Sawyer asks, calling my attention back to the present-day him. I'm not sure whether that's a good thing or not.

"I think we have the power needed," I respond. "But whether or not the spell works in the first place is another matter." I take a sip of the coffee. It's perfect, not that I'm surprised. I think the only thing that would take me even more off guard at this point is if he'd gotten it from Willow's shop, but I doubt that. I'd have a dozen texts right now if he'd turned up there.

"Hmm. True. It's old and there are no reports about what happened when the previous curse breaker tried to use it."

"When was that?"

"Three centuries ago in Scotland. It was an unsuccessful study of a stone close to the fae academy up there."

"I don't imagine the fae were very accomodating to a witch and a necromancer traipsing about their land."

"Not according to the site reports, no."

"We'll try," I decide. "The worst that happens is that we can't do it."

"Or the stone swears it's going to get vengeance on us."

A soft snort of amusement escapes from me. "I'm reasonably sure it's already done that. It's punishing me already by making the site unworkable. I can't put my team in danger by letting them continue to work on this case."

He nods in understanding. "But you don't want to stop..."

"If this doesn't work, then I'm going to have to," I point out.

"There's no shame in that." The earnest note to his words cuts through everything else. "Everyone has a failed dig to their name."

"I know. But how long is this going to bother me for?"

"Until you make your next discovery," he teases.

"Somehow, I don't think that's going to be the case. This stone is going to haunt me for the rest of my life."

A small smile lifts the corners of his lips. "Maybe. But as you said yourself, there's a good chance that's already the case."

"Eurgh, don't repeat me back to me. It sucks to be

right." I slurp down the rest of my coffee and slip the cup into one of the recycling bins scattered around the camp. "Let's get this over with."

"I thought you'd be more excited about it," Sawyer says.

"I'll be extra excited if it works," I promise.

"That's fair."

We make our way over to the stone in companionable silence. I imagine both of us are lost in our own thoughts about what's going to happen when we attempt this spell. We've never combined our magic before. In fact, I've never combined my magic with anyone before. Necromancers are private in nature about their magic, and I'm no different.

The stone taunts me from its grassy perch.

Or maybe it doesn't and I'm starting to imagine it. As much as I don't want to admit it, everyone's insistence that the stone is doing things and causing most of the problems we're having, I don't *want* to believe it. But that doesn't mean I'm not going to have to accept it.

"Are you ready?" Sawyer asks me, pulling his wand out.

I chew my bottom lip, trying to work out what the answer to that is. I don't think I'd ever be ready for this. Sharing magic with anyone is considered intimate, but with an ex-boyfriend...maybe it's best if I don't think about some of the implications of what we're about to do.

"You need to push your magic into me, and then I'll direct it from my wand," he says.

I nod as I reach out to place a hand on his arm. Technically, we don't have to touch for this to work, but it removes an unnecessary barrier we'd be faced with otherwise.

I close my eyes and focus on my thoughts and memories about Sawyer. It's a dangerous thing for me to do when it comes to my heart, but it's the only way we'll be able to form the connection to share magic.

Glimpses of us together flash through my mind. Our first kiss, the date at the fair where he got a nosebleed, the night we first slept together...

Sawyer clears his throat. "Am I supposed to be seeing this?"

Embarrassment floods through me. "I don't know," I admit. "I've never done this before."

"Okay, I'll try not to let it distract me."

"And I'll try to block the images from getting through."

"I don't mind too much," he responds with a

teasing note in his voice. "It's nice to know what you think of me."

"Maybe I should think of moments where I hated you," I mutter.

"Can you?"

"No." Which he knows well enough.

We stop talking so I can focus again. This time, it isn't memories, but imagining what it would be like to kiss him now. Or do more. Maybe in the tent over there...

No. I can't think about that, even if the smugness coming from him suggests he isn't against the idea.

"Focus," I instruct him.

"It's a bit hard to when you're wondering if I've learned anything new and if you can put it to the test."

"Cast your spell, warlock," I growl.

He chuckles, but lifts his wand like he needs to.

An odd sensation of my magic travelling through me and him and being directed by the wand tugs at me. It's not what I expect it to be, and it's very different from what using my magic is normally like. But it's not as unpleasant as I expect it to be.

Our combined power covers the stone, glowing and dancing in the air. It's more beautiful than I expect. And entrancing. I wonder why more people haven't talked about this.

A giant crack sounds, sending a wave of horror through me. Have we broken the stone?

Before I can try to figure out the answer, we're thrown backwards. My connection with both Sawyer and the magic snaps like an elastic band, making me feel as if my insides have been completely shaken up. It's *not* a nice feeling.

Sawyer groans and rubs his head as he sits up. Thankfully, his wand is still in his other hand and seems to be undamaged by being flung a couple of feet.

"Are you okay?" he asks.

"Just bruised, I think," I assure him.

Slowly, I climb to my feet, with Sawyer doing the same beside me.

The stone sits completely untouched in the middle of the field. I don't need to do any more magic to know it's completely unaffected by what we just did.

"I'm starting to hate this stone," I mutter.

"You and me both," he agrees. "Why don't we go out for some dinner to cheer ourselves up?" he suggests.

"As friends?" I'm not sure what I want his answer to that to be.

"As a date," he corrects.

My heart skips a beat. It turns out I *do* know what I want him to say.

"I'm just going off what you were projecting at me," he says when I don't respond. "But if you're not comfortable..."

"I am. Comfortable I mean. I'd love to go on a date with you."

And I mean every word. The stone may not have gone my way, but at least this can. And I'd call that a win.

9

I DON'T WANT to admit how nervous I am to be sat across a table from Sawyer. It's been a long time since the two of us have been on a date. Or since I've been on a date at all. The pub we're in has even dimmed the lights since we sat down and ate our main meals.

"Do you want dessert?" he asks.

"I couldn't."

"They have warm chocolate brownies with ice cream. We can share one if you want?"

My heart skips a beat at the insinuation. And the twinkle in his eyes. It's almost as if he knows what the suggestion is going to do.

And it does sound delicious.

"Is that an excuse just to get me to sit closer to

you?" It's a moment before I realise I've said the words out loud and not just thought them.

Oops.

I'd blame the wine, but I haven't had any. I have to be up early tomorrow in order to supervise the disassembly of the camp and then finish writing up my report for the financial backers. I don't think they're going to be too impressed with the lack of dig, but they won't be able to argue when I present a case for how dangerous it is for us to continue.

"Maybe," he admits, flagging down a waitress and ordering before I have a chance to say no.

Not that I'm going to. And he knows me well enough to be able to tell that.

It barely takes five minutes for our dessert to arrive. The brownie is still steaming and the ice cream on top has started to melt, seeping into it and making it extra delicious, just the way I like it. There are even two spoons already propped onto the side of the dish.

I don't wait for Sawyer to invite me to move closer and shuffle around so there's barely an inch between us, but I make sure to leave at least that. I don't want to be too distracted by the way it feels to be close to him, though I'm starting to suspect it's too late for that.

He picks up his spoon and digs in. "Mmm, this is good. You're going to love it," he says.

I relax a little and grab the extra spoon, pushing it through the dense chocolatey goodness. I'm glad he ordered it, and not just because it's got us sitting closer together than before, which I like more than I want to admit, even to myself.

"I need to have this again, sometime," he announces, turning to me with a boyish grin stretched over his face and a dot of chocolate sauce just below his lips.

"You have dessert on your chin," I say, tapping the position on my own face.

"Oh." He wipes it on his sleeve, only making it worse.

"No luck. Can I?"

He nods.

I pick up one of the spare napkins from our table and lean in, wiping it against his chin tenderly. I don't pull my hand away when I'm done, my atten- tion completely locked on him. I swallow, trying to ignore the way my gaze is being constantly pulled to his lips.

I wonder if they feel the same way I remember them doing. Gentle and caring, with a hint of unre- strained passion underneath, but only when he knew for sure that I was on board with it. He knew how to make me feel like I was the one in control.

The memories float close to the surface, making me bite my bottom lip.

A soft groan comes from Sawyer and he closes his eyes.

"Don't do that," he whispers.

I startle. "Do what? Sorry." I pull my hand back and drop the napkin to the table.

"Bite your lip. You know what it does to me."

"Still?" I don't know why I'm surprised. He's still having the same effect on me as he used to. It shouldn't be too much of a surprise that he's feeling the same way I am. We've both been part of the same situations over the past week.

He clears his throat. "Honestly? Yes. If you'd asked me a couple of weeks ago if it would, I'd have said no. But being around you..." he trails off.

"It's brought it all back," I finish for him. "For me too. I didn't realise how much I've missed you until you were there to show me." The floodgates have opened and there's no way for me to get my feelings back inside.

Sawyer reaches out and touches my cheek, his touch as gentle as ever. He leans in, the promise in his eyes making me bite my lip once more.

"Sabine..." There's so much want in his voice that it's impossible to ignore.

"Kiss me," I whisper. "Please."

Ah. I sound as if I want this just as much as he does. Probably because I do. There's no way either of us can resist now we've come as far as this.

He doesn't need any more invitation than that, and presses his lips against mine.

Just like I remember, his touch is gentle at first, but there's an assertiveness underneath that he didn't have before. I don't know if it's something he's gained with age, or if it's because he knows how much he wants me.

I wrap my arms around his neck and pull him closer, deepening the kiss. I'm desperate for more, to consume every part of him. We have plenty still to work out if we want this to work, but none of that is of any particular concern right now. The *only* thing that matters is the way he's making me feel and the connection that has always existed between the two of us.

We break apart, both breathing heavily, neither of us able to say a word.

My lips tingle from the echo of his touch. I lift my fingers to them, but they don't feel any different.

"Was it always as good as that?" he murmurs.

"In my memory, it is," I admit.

"You think about us?"

"All the time. I'll be in the middle of a dig and I'll see something that you'd find interesting, and I'll spend the rest of the day thinking about what I'd tell you about it." But he's never been there. I've never had anyone to actually tell it to.

"I do the same when I find something that needs investigating and I think it would be perfect for you," he admits sheepishly. "I'm not ready to lose you again."

"You don't have to." The words are out almost instantly, but I don't mind. I mean them. "I'm not sure how the future is going to look, but I know we can make it work this time."

"Me too." He leans in and kisses me again.

I lose myself in Sawyer. In something that's both old and new, familiar and exciting.

This time, things will end differently for us, I'm sure of it.

ONE WEEK LATER

THE TWO OF us look out at the stone, studying it intently.

"Maybe it's just a rock after all," I say, trying not to let my disappointment get to me too much. Excavations like this happen sometimes, there's nothing anyone can do about them.

It doesn't stop the pang of sadness travelling through me as a result. I don't like to fail.

"If you think about it, this isn't a loss," Sawyer says.

"How so?"

"I could say something cheesy about how we've

reconnected and managed to rekindle our relationship, but I know you won't accept that as an answer."

A small smile twists at my lips. "That's a personal
success, not a professional one."

"I know. That's why I'm not going to say that."

"I'm not following." I'm sure he's going to have a
dazzling answer about the excavation, but I can't for
the death of me think about what it could be.

"You can add to the legend of the Humber Stone,"
he says. "Everyone has their theories about what it is,
and you can add yours to it too."

"Except that I'm an archaeologist, I deal in what's
presented to me, not what I can make up to explain
things."

"You *can* rely on what's been in front of you,
though," he counters. "You'll have to report all of the
things that happened and went wrong and you can
put it down to the stone. Everyone else is going to
when they tell their friends and family anyway."

"It *could* have been the stone."

"But even admitting that much is going to add to
the legends of the stone. There'll be legends of
Sabine Bell, the woman who tried to discover the
truth about the stone and found that it was an old
magical item of immense power. There's no lie
there."

"You've been working at the DMH too long."

"How so?"

"You've learned how to make things pretty, even when they aren't."

He chuckles. "Well, the sites we manage do have to attract people to them if we want to keep up with our funding needs."

"Your work sounds *exhilarating*."

"I could say the same about your paperwork. There are parts of every job that we're not going to like, even the best one in the world."

"Hmm. True," I agree, but not without a little hesitance.

"But even before I came here I was thinking it might be time for a career change."

"And a little adventure?" Hope blooms within me. Maybe I'll get my dream from when we met after all.

"Or a lot of adventure. How would you feel about taking me with you next time you have an excavation?"

"Hmm. I'll have to check with the boss, she's very particular about who joins her team." I tap my chin.

"And hopefully, very persuadable." He tugs me around and pulls me to him.

I let out a carefree laugh. I'm not sure I've made a sound like that in years.

He leans in and captures my lips with his, kissing me deeply and making me certain of how serious he is about what he's saying. He really does want to come with me on my next excavation.

And hopefully the one after that too.

I melt into him, encouraging the kiss to go on for longer than is proper considering we're in the middle of camp. All around us, people are striking down tents and packing up expensive equipment carefully. We should probably be helping rather than kissing one another.

But I don't care. I've given a lot of myself to my job, now it's time for me to take a little for myself.

We break apart, the world seeping back in slowly.

"Keep going like you are, and she'll probably be saying yes by nightfall."

"I hope she's screaming it," he teases.

I make a fake shocked noise. "Maybe she will, but I can't make any guarantees."

A mischievous twinkle enters his eyes. "Then it's a good job I can."

I shake my head in bemusement, secretly liking the way he's making me feel. Or maybe not so secretly, I'm reasonably sure he's able to tell by the way I respond to him.

"Is it weird that even though this is one of my

biggest professional failures, I'm kind of fond of the rock?" I ask as I pull away from him and turn back to the stone.

"It makes sense to me. It's easily the best stone I've ever tried to crack the mysteries of."

I resist the urge to roll my eyes.

"We should go. They're nearly done taking everything down."

He nods. "How long do you have before your next excavation starts?"

"A couple of weeks, but I might be able to delay it a bit longer if you want to spend a little bit more time together," I suggest with a note of hope in my voice.

"That sounds nice. It'll be good to see Willow again too."

I chuckle. "Prepare for a barrage of questions. She's excited."

"She's always been excited about everything. I don't think she needs to drink coffee to have a pep in her step."

"You're not wrong," I agree. It's good that he already knows my best friend. And she him, it makes it all that little bit easier to manage.

"Shall we?" he asks, holding out his arm for me to take.

I slip my own through and rest my hand on his sleeve. As I turn away from the source of all my frustration, something magical catches my eye. I spin around to get a better look, but nothing is there.

"Sabine? Is everything all right?" Sawyer asks.

"Yes, it's nothing."

Some mysteries are better left unsolved, and I think the Humber Stone is one of them.

Thank you for reading *Unfortunate Decrees and Iced Coffees,* I hope you enjoyed it! Sabine will appear in the *Cauldron Coffee Shop* series which follows her best friend, Willow, as she uncovers the truth about the mysterious (and jealous) teapot. It starts with *Pumpkin Spice And All Things Nice:* http:// books2read.com/pumpkinspiceandallthingsnice

Thank you for reading *Unfortunate Decrees And Iced Coffees*, I hope you enjoyed it! This is a prequel to the series surrounding Sabine's best friend, Willow, and a mysterious teapot found on one of her digs (if you want to find out more about the dig in question, you can in *This Time Is Trouble*!)

If you read the story in the Love and Legends anthology originally, then you may already know how some aspects of the story came to be! When my close friend and sometimes co-author, Skye MacKinnon, got herself a map of British Mythology, she decided that we *had* to run an anthology where everyone was assigned a random British myth and their story had to feature it (we can be quirky like that!) I made absolutely no plans for my myth beforehand, mostly because there was no way I could know what I'd get.

And then I got the Humber Stone. I still have no idea what it is. No one does - which is a bit of a problem if you want to write a story about it. Until I remembered that I already planned to write a story for Sabine, my necromancer archaeologist, as a side story for the *Cauldron Coffee Shop* series. And so my story became linked to the fact no one knows what the Humber Stone is or does (other than bring bad luck). One of the reasons I decided not to have Sabine discover the truth about the Humber Stone herself is because of the mystery around what this stone is. I thought it would be most in keeping with the legend.

As for Sabine, she's named after a very dear friend of mine who once lamented to me that there were never any "good guys" named Sabine, they were always evil - hopefully, I fixed that so there's at least one good Sabine in literature!

Finally, if you want to get to know Mona, you can in the complete *Grimalkin Academy: Kittens* series, which starts with *First Time's A Charm*.

If you want to keep up to date with new releases

and other news, you can join my Facebook Reader Group or mailing list.

Stay safe & happy reading!

- Laura

- The Shifter Season
- Cauldron Coffee Shop
- Obscure Academy

The Forgotten Gods World

- The Queen of Gods*
- Forgotten Gods
- Forgotten Gods: Origins

The Grimm World

- Grimm Academy*
- Fate Of The Crown*
- Once Upon An Academy Series

The Paranormal Council Universe

- The Paranormal Council Series
- The Fae Queen Of Winter Trilogy*
- Paranormal Criminal Investigations
- MatchMater Paranormal Dating App*
- The Necromancer Council*
- Return Of The Fae*

Other Series

- The Apprentice Of Anubis
- Beyond The Curse
- Untold Tales*
- The Dragon Duels*
- Rosewood Academy
- ME*
- Seven Wardens*, co-written with Skye MacKinnon
- Tales Of Clan Robbins, co-written with L.A. Boruff
- Firehouse Witches*, co-written with Lacey Carter Andersen & L.A. Boruff
- Purple Oasis, co-created series with Arizona Tape

Twin Souls Universe, all series co-written with Arizona Tape

- Twin Souls*
- Dragon Soul*
- The Renegade Dragons*
- The Vampire Detective*
- Amethyst's Wand Shop Mysteries

Mountain Shifters Universe, all series co-written with L.A. Boruff

- Valentine Pride*
- Magic and Metaphysics Academy*

Audiobooks: www.authorlauragreenwood.co.uk/p/audio.html

- Facebook Group: http://facebook.com/groups/theparanormalcouncil
- Facebook Page: http://facebook.com/authorlauragreenwood
- Bookbub: www.bookbub.com/authors/laura-greenwood

www.ingramcontent.com/pod-product-compliance
Lightning Source LLC
Chambersburg PA
CBHW031754150726
47989CB00006B/2713